Zoë
and the
Magic Harp

Jane Andrews

Piccadilly Press • London

It was the evening of the annual Fairy Ball in the Fairy Queen's castle. All the fairies were dancing to the wonderful music, played by the Fairy Queen on her magic golden harp. The harp's magic was very strong and only the Fairy Queen could play it. If anyone else tried, a spell would be cast over them.

Zoë
and the
Magic Harp

For Sophie

First published in Great Britain in 2004
by Piccadilly Press Ltd.,
5 Castle Road, London NW1 8PR
www.piccadillypress.co.uk

Text and illustration copyright © Jane Andrews, 2004

Text and cover designed by Louise Millar
Printed and bound in Belgium by Proost

ISBN: 1 85340 749 6 (hardback)
1 85340 744 5 (paperback)

1 3 5 7 9 10 8 6 4 2

A catalogue record of this book
is available from the British Library

Jane Andrews has two sons and lives in High Wycombe in Buckinghamshire.
Piccadilly Press also publish the other books in this series:
**Zoë at Fairy School, Zoë the Tooth Fairy, Zoë and the Fairy Crown,
Zoë and the Witches' Spell** and **Zoë and the Dragon**

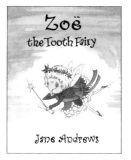

ISBN: 1 85340 640 6 (p/b)   ISBN: 1 85340 651 1 (p/b)   ISBN: 1 85340 644 9 (p/b)   ISBN: 1 85340 726 7 (p/b)   ISBN: 1 85340 728 3 (p/b)

No one saw two little witches who had come to spy
on the celebration.
The witches were planning a secret midnight feast, and when
they heard the beautiful music the Fairy Queen was playing,
they decided to steal the harp for their own party . . .

When the ball was over and the lights had gone out, the two witches crept out of their hiding place and together they picked up the harp. But the harp was heavy and difficult to carry, and it made a loud *clang!* as it hit the windowsill.

Zoë and Pip heard the noise and rushed back to the ballroom to see what had happened.

"Quick!" Zoë whispered as she caught sight of the witches climbing on to their broomsticks. "We must get the harp back!"

Both fairies flew out into the night as fast as they could. They tried with all their might to catch the witches, but the witches' broomsticks were much faster than their fairy wings.

"We need broomsticks too," said Pip, panting.

Zoë and Pip fell further and further behind as they chased the witches to the castle, which was nestled in the dark and scary forest below.

As the fairies approached, they saw a ghostly light shining through one of the windows and flew down to investigate.

Through the window, Zoë and Pip could see all the little witches having their midnight feast. They were eating spider cookies and drinking mud cocoa, and in the centre of the room was . . .

. . . the Fairy Queen's magic harp!
"We must find a way into the castle and rescue
the harp!" whispered Zoë.

They tried a small door but it was very cross and it wouldn't let them through.

They tried some windows, but the windows blew them away.

They flew round and round and higher and higher until eventually they found a tiny little window open at the top of one of the castle's towers, and Zoë and Pip squeezed through.

But horrors! As soon as they made it through the window, they started sliding very fast down a dark, long, winding chute! They fell deeper and deeper into the castle and landed at the bottom with a big bump. Zoë and Pip dusted themselves off and began their search.

It wasn't long before they heard some excited chatter coming from a nearby room, and through the half-open door, they could see the ghostly light again.

The feast was over. "On your feet! It's time to dance!" cried Mo. Tabitha sat down to play the harp and plucked a string.

With a sharp *twang!* and a shower of sparks,
the string snapped in two, and . . .

. . . each and every little witch froze like a statue!
"Quick, let's get the harp!" said Pip.
"No," said Zoë. "The magic has been released –
We mustn't touch it! Let's go back
and get the Fairy Queen."

When Zoë and Pip finally arrived back at the castle, the Fairy Queen was fast asleep in her bed. They stood outside her door for some time before knocking. The Fairy Queen did not like being woken up in the middle of the night.

"Who's there?" the Fairy Queen asked grumpily when they knocked for a third time.

But when Zoë and Pip explained what had happened, she immediately grabbed her phone and made a call.

The Head Witch was enjoying her nightly broomstick ride and was not pleased when her mobile rang.

"Nonsense!" she protested. "They were all asleep when I left."

"Well," the Fairy Queen informed her crossly, "at the moment they are all frozen in your dining hall with my harp! We're on our way. Be there!"

The Head Witch flew back home as fast as she could.

The dining hall in the witches' castle looked a sorry sight indeed.
Some of the witches were frozen in very funny positions.
"I've a good mind to leave you this way!" scolded the Head Witch.
Zoë and Pip tried hard not to giggle.

"The least they could do is return my harp," said the Fairy Queen.
The Head Witch moved away to allow the Fairy Queen to
perform her spell to release the witches.

The Head Witch lined the little witches up. "No pudding for any of you for a long time!" she said. "And I believe I know who is responsible for this . . ."
She turned and pointed her long finger directly at Tabitha and Mo.

"Tabitha and Mo, you will hand your broomsticks over to Zoë and Pip for one full month! I'm certain they will have good fun looking after them for you."

"Yippee!" cheered Zoë and Pip, and they raced off ahead of the Fairy Queen, like two rockets into the night sky.

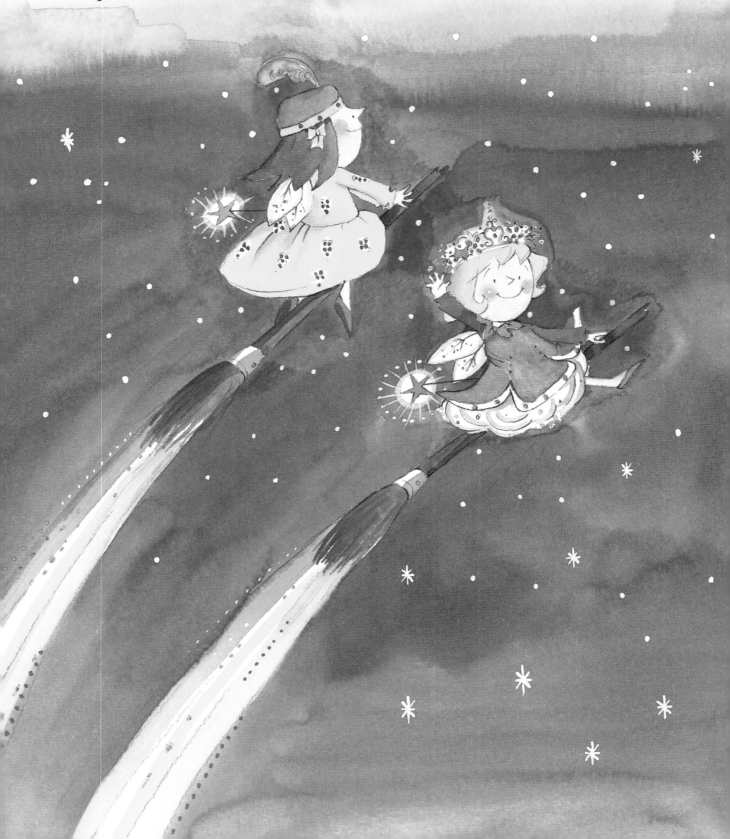